偽 textbook English
英語教科書

"Uncooked barley, uncooked rice, uncooked egg! Yeah!"

English
偽 英語教科書
全民英檢不會考、學校不敢教、背了也說不出口的單字&片語

作　　者／中山
插　　畫／千野A
譯　　者／錢亞東

發 行 人／黃鎮隆
協　　理／陳君平
資深主編／袁珮玲
美術總監／沙雲佩
封面設計／陳碧雲
公關宣傳／邱小祐、陶若瑤

出　　版／城邦文化事業股份有限公司　尖端出版
　　　　　台北市民生東路二段141號10樓
　　　　　電話：(02)2500-7600　傳真：(02)2500-1975
　　　　　讀者服務信箱：spp_books@mail2.spp.com.tw
發　　行／英屬蓋曼群島商家庭傳媒股份有限公司
　　　　　城邦分公司　尖端出版
　　　　　台北市民生東路二段141號10樓
　　　　　電話：(02)2500-7600(代表號)　傳真：(02)2500-1979
　　　　　劃撥專線：(03)312-4212
　　　　　劃撥戶名：英屬蓋曼群島商家庭傳媒(股)公司城邦分公司
　　　　　劃撥帳號：50003021
　　　　　※劃撥金額未滿500元，請加付掛號郵資50元
法律顧問／通律機構　台北市重慶南路二段59號11樓

台灣地區總經銷／中彰投以北(含宜花東)　高見文化行銷股份有限公司
　　　　　　　　電話：0800-055-365　傳真：(02)2668-6220
　　　　　　　　雲嘉以南　威信圖書有限公司
　　　　　　　　(嘉義公司)電話：0800-028-028　傳真：(05)233-3863
　　　　　　　　(高雄公司)電話：0800-028-028　傳真：(07)373-0087
馬新地區總經銷／城邦(馬新)出版集團　Cite(M) Sdn.Bhd.(458372U)
　　　　　　　　電話：(603)9057-8822、9056-3833　傳真：(603)9057-6622
　　　　　　　　E-mail：cite@cite.com.my
　　　　　　　　大眾書局(新加坡)　POPULAR(Singapore)
　　　　　　　　電話：65-6462-9555　傳真：65-6468-3710
　　　　　　　　E-mail：feedback@popularworld.com
　　　　　　　　大眾書局(馬來西亞)　POPULAR(Malaysia)
　　　　　　　　電話：603-9179-6333　傳真：03-9179-6200、03-9179-6339
　　　　　　　　客服諮詢熱線：1-300-88-6336
　　　　　　　　E-mail：popularmalaysia@popularworld.com

版　　次／2014年11月初版　Printed in Taiwan　ISBN 978-957-10-5733-0

國家圖書館出版品預行編目資料

偽英語教科書：全民英檢不會考、學校不敢
教、背了也說不出口的單字&片語／中山 著 --
初版 --臺北市：尖端, 2014.11
　面；公分
　ISBN 978-957-10-5733-0(平裝)
1. 英語　2. 詞彙
805.12　　　　　　　　　　103016721

前言

本書不是以立志考「多益TOEIC」、「英語能力檢定」等英文資格考試的考生為對象，而是將Twitter上面發表的「多讀無益TOEIC英文單字」的內容編輯成書。

在大家一開口就會說英語、全球扁平化的今天，做為國際社會交流工具的「英語」其重要性只有與日俱增，英語裡的文化教養對於商務人士來說更是成為必要的條件。在這種因勢利導的局面下，愈來愈多企業都將TOEIC的資格考成績列為升等要件，資格考試將決定你今後的薪資和升官，搞得事情變得很大條。在龐大的日常業務和責任制加班之外，週末還要和客戶應酬、陪妻小遊玩；對於蠟燭多頭燒的上班族而言，心中是多麼渴望有一本能在短時間內就可有效應付考試的教材。

如果要肩負起滿足這時代和社會的偉大任務，本書自願承讓給其他更有來頭的出版品，反道其道而行立志成為「最不實用的教材」。為什麼「反其道而行」，其實本人也不清楚。正如古有明訓：「先將護城河填平（一步一腳印之意）」、「射將先射馬（擒賊先擒王之意）」，這些都是日本古代武士們為了達成目標所採用的做事流程；我把這些流程曲解掉後，好像就有那麼一點歪打正著離目標更近的感覺出來了，你說對不對？有一說是英文單字數量有幾百萬個之多，TOEIC要考到900分以上至少必須具備其中的15000個單字量，所以我們必須填平的護城河溝太深了、要射掉的馬也太多了；但是，只要敵人愈強大，我方就熊熊燃燒得愈起勁，這才是從小看《週刊少年JUMP》長大的21世紀企業戰士該有的抱負啊！

這次，非常感謝居然願意接納我這超冷想法的出版社編輯品川、設計出這麼好看書籍的木庭、簡直是搏性命在畫這150張插畫的千野、擔任英文文法檢查和配音的山繆先生，以及The Geese的尾關。當然，更要感謝一書在手粉絲們的支持。

鈴木先生

西村先生

木村先生
和下山先生

克莉絲蒂
全美第一綜合
醫院的選秀第一
順位指名護士。
身高190cm，
體重80kg的內科手。
金臂人。

鮑伯
他是天才還是天然呆？
即使犯下出槌的大烏龍，
也能用笑臉化解的幸運兒。
在太平盛世是奸臣，
在亂世中還是奸臣。
右投右奸臣。
興趣是替人開心導管
手術的業餘玩家。

副主任
耗在三千煩惱絲上的青春。
大部分的收入
都花在生髮劑上，
孤傲的發毛藝術家。

櫃台小姐
會長在泰國浴
親自三顧「毛」廬
才請回來的派遣社員。
基本上來説只當花瓶。

會計課長
打算計機訓練出的
金手指，拿來應用在
性技巧上，是會「技」部
叫我第一名的晚班
「技」算師。
42歲，處男。

人物介紹
CHARACTERS

部門經理
愈老愈鳥來伯。
加州的虎眼石都被他的
性慾洗成結石。

諸葛亮
蜀漢的軍師。

董事長
從一個
暴露狂白手起家。
社訓是「不要使用咒語」。

史蒂芬妮的母親
因為雞毛蒜皮小事
而造成精神崩潰，
在現實與精神世界中徘徊的
「來去哈娃姨」。

史蒂芬妮
原本只有
「淡淡的蠢蠢欲動」，
後來搞到衣服全脫的
神經質變態女人。
要在男性社會生存下去，
必須要有亞馬遜
女人國的源流
和純文學打底，
具有複雜的
思考回路。

路人甲
要去新宿車站
居然東耗西耗了3年，
一直在東京都內遊蕩的變態。
HP60．MP12。

齊藤先生

赤松氏
以很瞎的學說在學會裡
掀起爆笑的
不靠譜教授，
到底有沒有
博士學位令人質疑。

目錄

CHAPTER 1

絕對
不會出題的
英文單字

THE FIRST 50 NONESSENTIAL VOCABULARY
Encounter Rate 0%

001

salmon carpaccio

［生鮭魚片］

例句

鮑伯笑得太厲害，
居然從鼻孔中噴出了生鮭魚片。

Bob laughed so hard that the salmon carpaccio
came out of his nose.

☞ 真的噴得出來吼！意外的還是完整一片。

002

dump

［大便］

例句

史蒂芬妮在公司裡
故意不把大便沖掉。

After taking a dump at work,
Stefanie doesn't flush the toilet on purpose.

☞ 這絕對是人見人怕的恐怖攻擊。

003

pillow talk

［枕邊細語］

例句

說起枕邊細語，
敝公司的會計課長無人能出其右。

When it comes to pillow talk,
the account general could rival anyone.

☞ 晚上也要做會計（技）工作？人家不知道意思啦！

004

horny

［想嘿咻］

例句

「我有點想嘿咻了，
可以先下班回家嗎？」

"May I go home early?
I'm feeling rather horny."

☞ 如果下面開始蠢蠢欲動或想愛愛時要趕快回家才行。

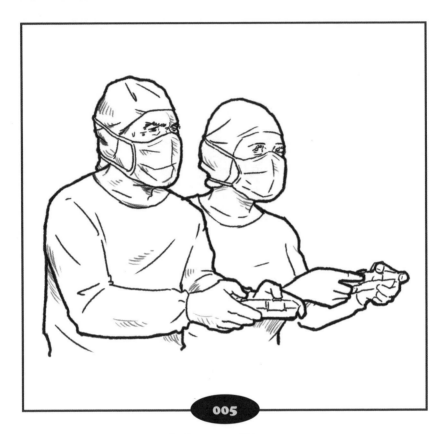

005

Mario Kart

［瑪利歐賽車］

例句

「瑪利歐賽車就先打到這好了，
繼續動手術吧！」

"Enough Mario Kart,
let's resume surgery."

☞ 手術中的遊戲一天打一小時就好，任何事適可而止最重要。

006

dirty joke
［黃色笑話］

例句

「經理的超殺黃色笑話，把春酒變成花酒了。」

The New Year celebration was completely ruined
by the manager's dirty jokes.

☞ 到底說了什麼有「射」笑話？
他正經的表情很難想像居然會是黃帝。

007

nipple
［乳頭］

例句

「為什麼妳要玩乳頭？」
「因為乳不在高，有頭則靈。」

"Why do you fiddle with the nipple?"
"Because it's there."

☞ 不要用頭來理解，要用身體去感受。

008

completely naked
［全裸的］

例句

部門經理全裸的跑去追聖誕老人。
The department manager tried to tackle the Santa Claus
while completely naked.

☞ 到底是經理會先追到聖誕老人？還是警察會先抓到經理？
這對優秀的警察來說真是一大挑戰！

009

quadruple jump

［四回轉跳］

例句

他是全世界四回轉跳中
唯一的暴露狂。

He is the only exhibitionist
to execute a quadruple jump.

☞ 少有的可造廢才，要好好栽培才行。

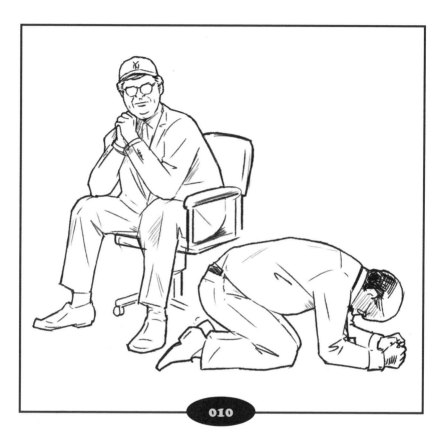

010

erogenous zone

［性感帶］

例句

鮑伯和客戶會商時，
無巧不巧發現了客戶的性感帶。

Bob accidentally found a client's erogenous zone
in the business meeting.

☞ 無巧不巧真是註衰的一件事。

011

char siu

［叉燒］

例句

業務部同仁在吃叉燒前，
要先得到上司的批准才行。

Sales department members must obtain permission
from their supervisors before eating char siu.

☞ 滷蛋嫩不嫩在現場直接戳破就知，
但叉燒還是要老臉皮的上司判斷才行啊！

ponzu sauce

［柚子醋］

例句

「老闆，這不是你要的合約，是柚子醋。」
「哎呀！」

"Boss, this isn't the contract. It's ponzu sauce."
"Oops!"

☞ 如果是反過來的情況就更少見了，
這官大真的就學問大嗎？

013

sexual slave

［性奴隸］

例句

「課長，2線是你的性奴隸打來的。」
「好的，我來接。」

"Boss, your sexual slave is on line 2."
"Thank you."

☞ 輕描淡寫就把公私混為一談。

014

raise an army

[舉兵]

例句

2011年6月，
副理在九州舉兵起義。

In June 2011,
the assistant manager raised an army in Kyusyu.

☞ 名古屋分社總裁也要響應嗎？

015

army crawl

［匍匐前進］

例句

「今晚要不要一起匍匐前進？
我在車站附近找到一個危險地帶喲！」

"Could you do an army crawl with me past the station tonight?
It's dangerous there."

☞ 下班後來一趟匍匐前進，是上班族最大的享受。

016

chainsaw

［電鋸］

例句

櫃台小姐整個上午
都一直在用電鋸工作。

The lady at the reception desk works
with a chainsaw all morning.

☞ 櫃台如戰場，來一個鋸一個。

23

017

panty line

［內褲痕］

例句

為了廣大的後生晚輩，
可以讓我看妳的內褲痕嗎？

"Just for future reference,
may I check your panty line?"

☞ 什麼後生晚輩，所以是要從後面來嗎？

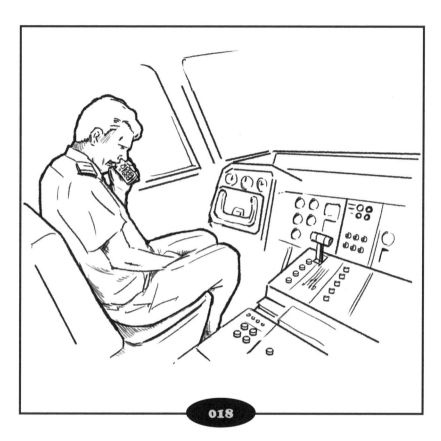

018

women issues

［桃色糾紛］

例句

「機上的旅客請注意，
因為機長的桃色糾紛，
飛往波昂的786班機將延後起飛。」

"Attention, please. Flight 786 to Bonn has been delayed
as the captain is having women issues."

☞ 安全的飛航之旅，有任何一絲差池都不行的。

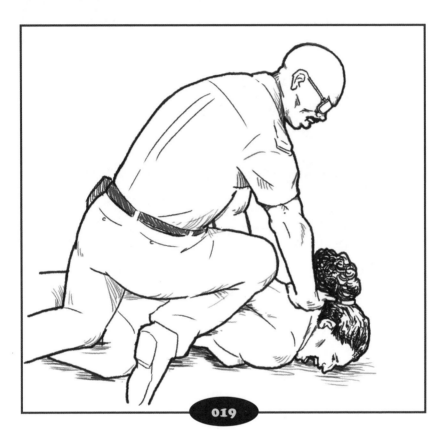

019

anus

［屁眼］

例句

新來的護士克莉絲蒂在手術進行中
隨便玩弄患者的屁眼，
遭到制伏在地。

During the operation, new nurse Kristi was caught touching
the patient's anus without reason.

☞ 真的是一疏忽手指就會趁隙而入。不過將她制伏的又是什麼人呢？

020

hangnail

［指甲肉刺］

例句

「女士先生們，
將你們的指甲肉刺剝下來吧！」

"Ladies and gentlemen, let's remove a hangnail."

☞ 把剝下來的肉刺收集起來，
送到聯合國兒童基金會來表達我們的心聲！

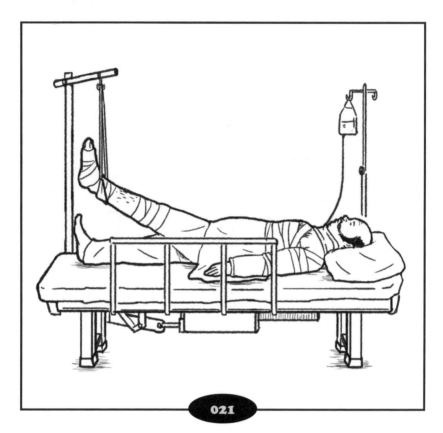

021

sexual position
[體位]

例句

部門經理在嘗試新體位時受到重傷，結果住院了。

The department manager is now in hospital after seriously injuring himself attempting a new sexual position.

☞ 勝敗乃兵家常事。挑戰九重天，方為人上人。

28

022

STD

［性病］

例句

在全員大會上，
CEO 向大家坦白
他得到性病的苦惱。

Our CEO expressed his worries about STDs
to all the staff in the assembly.

☞ 在向員工坦白前，請先向醫生坦白！

023

Kafrizzle

［火焰魔法］

例句

部門經理37歲時學會火焰魔法。

The department manager learns Kafrizzle at age 37.

☞ 這麼年輕就學會，將來打魔王時一定能派上用場。

024

briefs

［內褲］

例句

在創立紀念日上，辦公室懸掛了
12000件五顏六色的內褲。

To celebrate the foundation's anniversary,
the entire office is covered with about 12,000 colourful briefs.

☞ 這是為了工作時能感受新的氣息而誕生的儀式。

大戰時曾經中斷，現在又重新「內」舉不避親了。

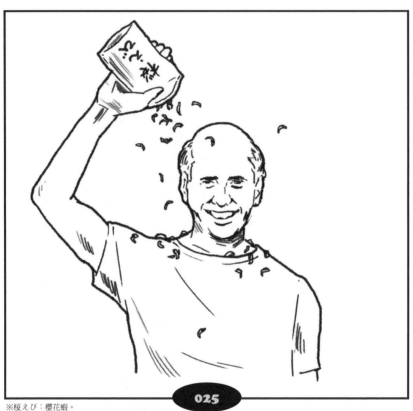

025

※桜えび：櫻花蝦。

sakura shrimp

［櫻花蝦］

例句

副主任為了促進生髮，
將櫻花蝦撒在頭上。

The deputy director sprinkles sakura shrimp
on his head to stimulate hair growth.

☞ 真是溺水者連稻草都要抓，禿頭者連櫻花蝦都不放過。

副主任的生髮工具
The Deputy Director's Hair-Growth Products

蕎麥麵粉 buckwheat flour
青汁 green juice
楓糖漿 maple syrup
發泡燒酒 Awamori
食用辣油 edible chili oil
樟腦丸 boric acid dumpling
硬碟 hard disk
海葵 sea anemone

脫毛劑 depilatory
托卡列夫手槍 Tokarev
鈾 uranium
水螅 polyp
軍師 military advisor
女人的第六感 women's intuition
孫子兵法 Sun-Tzu's The Art of War
大和魂 Japanese spirit

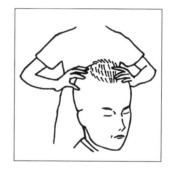

奧利奧餅乾 OREO
梵谷向日葵 Van Gogh's Sunflower
時間與空間 time and space
新自由主義 neoliberalism
關關同立① KANKANDORITSU
隼鷹 Hayabusa
快速通關証 Fastpass
RiUP生髮劑 RiUP

[註①]日本很難考上的關西大學、關西學院大學、同志社大學、立命館大學的四校總稱。

026

cosplay

［角色扮演］

例句

組長不知為何
角色扮演成部門經理的樣子。

For some reason the manager is cosplaying
as the department manager.

☞ 扮了之後心情很鬱卒，苦悶啊！

027

military advisor

［軍師］

例句

在那邊和史蒂芬妮跳舞的
打赤膊大叔是
劉備的軍師諸葛亮。

The topless man dancing over there with Stefanie
is Liu Bei's military advisor, Zhuge Liang.

☞「伏龍先生，你在這幹什麼？魏國已經打來了！」

028

big rod

［巨鵰］

例句

「先生，要怎麼稱呼您才好呢？」
「叫我巨鵰叔就好。」

"Mister, what would you like to be called?"
"I'd like to be called Big Rod."

☞「人家看不出哪裡有鳥……」

029

rain dance

［乞雨舞］

例句

「不好意思，她正在跳乞雨舞，暫時無法接聽您的電話。」

"I'm sorry, she can't come to the phone right now as she's doing a rain dance."

☞ 乾旱和工作電話，何者比較重要一目瞭然。

030

Thunder

［雷神］

例句

鮑伯偷偷把副理藏起來的雷神
換成七七乳加巧克力。

Bob secretly replaced the assistant manager's treasured
Thunder with NOUGAT CHOCOLATE.

☞ 該死！至少要鞭屍三百次才行。

031

pink rotor

［情趣按摩棒］

例句

「 在博愛座附近
請將情趣按摩棒的電源切掉。 」

"Please turn off your pink rotor
near the priority seat."

☞ 離博愛座很遠的地方也請切掉電源。

032

emiction

［排尿］

例句

「我要去洗手間，
你要看我排尿嗎？」

"I have to go to the restroom.
Will you keep an eye on my emiction for me?"

☞ 這已經是尿到病除的變態境界了。

033

bloomers

［女用燈籠褲］

例句

「你把女用燈籠褲罩在頭上要幹嘛？」
「今天有工作的面試。」

"What are you doing with bloomers on your head?"
"I'm going for a job interview today."

☞ 這真是打著燈籠也找不到的例子，請節哀。

034

erection

［勃起］

例句

尼克在研修期間一直勃起，
後來大家就叫他「富士山」。

Since maintaining an erection
throughout the duration of the training period,
Nick has been nicknamed "Fujiyama."

☞ 搭帳篷就叫富士山真是笑屎人了！
千萬不要小看我們露營者！

035

condom

［保險套］

例句

「這保險套看起來很棒，
但不知道合不合我的尺寸？」
「您要試穿看看嗎？」

"This is a good condom, but I wonder if it will fit me."
"Would you like to try it on?"

☞ 有這回事？更衣室的畫面肯定不堪入目。

036

fuck buddy

［炮友］

例句

「課長，2線是你炮友打來的。」
「好的，請接過來。」

"Boss, you have a call on line 2 from your fuck buddy."
"Thank you, put her through."

☞ 私情來時擋也擋不住，但是處理起來這麼日常也太屌了吧！

037

areola

［乳暈］

例句

「靠，鮑伯那混蛋！
乳暈大就跩個二五八萬的！」

"Geez, Bob sure has large areolas,
but does he need to be so bigheaded about it?"

☞ 就承認吧～令人羨慕吼！

038

chest hair

［胸毛］

例句

朝會之後，
CEO在茶水間裡邊哭邊拔胸毛。

After the morning assembly,
the CEO cried while plucking his chest hair in the kitchen.

☞ 在員工面前絕對不掉淚，真是經營者的好榜樣。

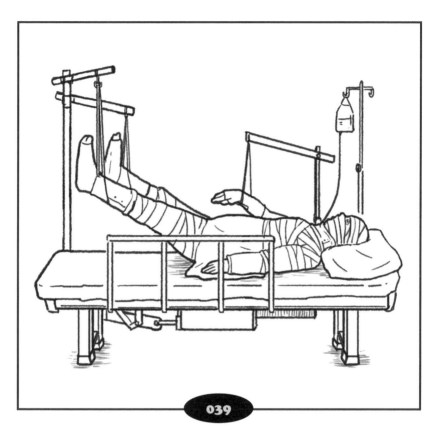

039

blindfold sex

[矇眼做愛]

例句

部門經理在挑戰矇眼做愛時又受重傷，再度住院了。

The department manager is now in hospital
after seriously injuring himself attempting blindfold sex.

☞ 到底是挑戰什麼高難度體位才會這麼嚴重？
勞健保不給付喔！

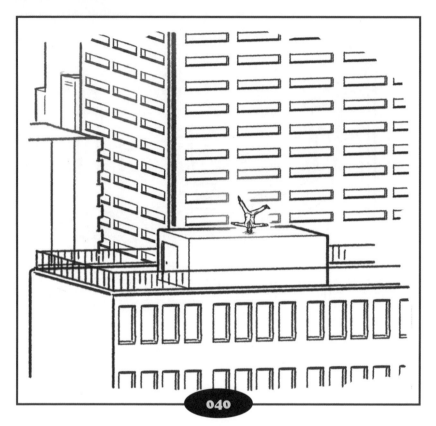

040

headspin

［頭轉］

例句

「在對面大樓用頭轉的老先生是誰？」
「是敝公司的董事長。」

"Who is that elderly gentleman over there doing a headspin?"
"Our chairman."

☞ 他為何而轉？以及在哪裡轉？
一定是有著凡人無法懂的深謀遠慮。

041

fart

［屁］

例句

父親的強烈臭屁
造成母親精神崩潰。

Dad's deadly fart caused our mother
to lose her mental balance.

☞ 是顏面直擊吧！

042

bottom cleavage

［股溝］

例句

「妳把顧客名單放哪裡去了？」
「我把它夾在組長的股溝裡了。」

"What did you do with the client list?"
"I inserted it into the section chief's bottom cleavage."

☞ 夾在那裡的，應該都是奧客的名單對吧？

043

run around naked

［裸奔］

例句

史蒂芬妮在辦公室裡裸奔要求加薪，但是被拒絕了。

Stefanie ran around the office naked and asked for a pay rise,
but the request was denied.

☞ 後來，形容努力卻無法得到回報的成語，
就叫「史無前『粒』」。

044

F-cup

[F 罩杯]

例句

F罩杯可以讓人升天，也可讓人窒息。

F-cups can help you or hurt you.

☞ 真是至理明言。但先生有事嗎？

045

mole hair

［痣毛］

例句

史蒂芬妮非常在意鮑伯的痣毛，
導致她睡不著。

Stefanie can't sleep
because she keeps thinking about Bob's mole hair.

☞ 到底要把痣毛拔掉？還是乾脆把鮑伯做掉？
人家好難抉擇喔！

046

masochist

［被虐狂］

例句

聽說行銷部門正在找
立馬就能派上戰場的被虐狂。

I heard that the marketing department
is looking for a work-ready masochist.

☞ 光從外表看來就挺嚇人的。
到底是行銷什麼啊？

047

stamp with blood

［血指印］

例句

「歹勢啦，郵差先生，找不到印章，蓋血指印可以嗎？」

"I'm sorry Mr. Postman, I can't find my personal seal.
Can I just stamp it with my blood?"

☞ 這樣子就要流血畫押，鐵打的身體也吃不消！

048

mistress

［小三］

例句

「感謝各位搭乘 Z 航空，
今天的機長是岡本桂，
我是他的小三草間俊子。」

"Thank you for flying Z airlines.
Your captain today is Kei Okamoto,
and I'm Toshiko Kusama, his mistress."

☞ 我們並不想跟你們一起共享翱翔於天際的樂趣。

049

Patriot missile

[愛國者飛彈]

例句

愛國者飛彈不可以放在兒童可以伸手搆到的地方。

Keep Patriot missiles out of the reach of children.

☞ 小屁孩最喜歡拿愛國者飛彈來玩了！

050

urine bottle

［尿壺］

例句

新手護士克莉絲蒂
用時速160公里將尿壺投了過來。

New nurse Kristi can throw a urine bottle
at 160 kilometers per hour.

☞ 為什麼要速投過來？捕手又是誰？
這謎團愈來愈深不可測了。

克莉絲蒂的金臂
Kristi Strong-arms

270 km/h

體溫計
clinical thermometer

副主任的生髮工具 2
The Deputy Director's Hair-Growth Products 2

使用前&使用後
Before & After

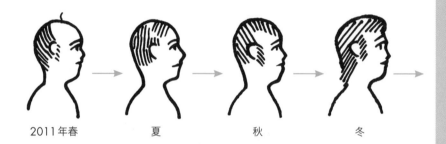

2011年春　　　　夏　　　　秋　　　　冬

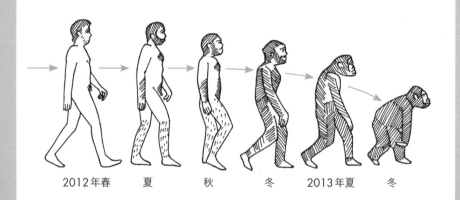

2012年春　　夏　　秋　　冬　　2013年夏　　冬

CHAPTER 2

很高機率不會考
的英文單字

THE SECOND 50 UNESSENTIAL VOCABULARY
Encounter Rate 5%

051

balls

［蛋蛋］

例句

諸葛孔明揮淚
踢馬謖的蛋蛋。

Weeping, Zhuge Liang kicked Ma Su in the balls.

☞ 揮淚斬馬稷，再加踹蛋蛋。

052

sexily

[性感地]

例句

為了閃避從馬路邊跳出來的假摔哥，
我性感地甩了方向盤。

I sexily swerved my car to avoid the boy
who had run into the road.

☞ 千鈞一髮還不忘賣弄性感，阿湯哥當如是也！

053

garter belt

［吊襪帶］

例句

「 在機長尚未將繫上吊襪帶的
指示燈熄滅前，
請不要解開吊襪帶。 」

"Please keep your garter belts fastened
until the captain has turned off the sign."

☞ 萬一有性感的緊急需要，隨時都要把它繫得緊緊的才行！

054

sensitive spot

［敏感部位］

例句

「已經『站起來』的乘客，
請抓住吊環或是
駕駛的敏感部位。」

"If you are standing, please hold on to the strap
or the driver's sensitive spot."

☞ 為了乘車的安全，不排除有臨時停車的可能性。

055

nipple cover

［胸貼］

例句

立花大師正在手作胸貼。
他是屋久島上僅存三位手感工匠的其中一位。

Mr. Tachibana is one of only three craftsmen
on Yakushima Island who makes nipple covers by hand.

☞ 工匠的技藝即將失傳，手作是強調「出自我手，貼在你胸」的觸感。

056

dine and dash

［吃霸王餐］

例句

服用這藥的前後30分鐘內，
請勿吃霸王餐。

Do not dine and dash for half an hour before
or after taking this medicine.

☞ 人生海海，霸王餐前請勿服用。

057

bungee

［高空彈跳］

例句

春天一到，部門經理就會從180米的
高台上進行高空彈跳。

Every spring, the department manager does a bungee jump
off a 180-meter high platform.

☞ 這是迎接春神到來的悠久傳統儀式。
春江水暖鴨先跳，管理級幹部就是要這樣！

058

pee

［尿尿］

例句

「啊，我要尿尿，快把那個碗拿過來！」

"Oh, I've got to pee. Pass me the bowl."

☞ 到底想幹嘛？

059

sexual propensity

[性癖]

例句

如有變更住址、電子信箱、
性癖的話，請通知我們。

Please keep us informed of any change of address,
e-mail address, or sexual propensity.

☞ 性癖是僅次於住址和電子信箱的重要情報嗎？

060

barium

［鋇］

例句

這是今天的主菜，
鋇的沙嗲。

"Today's main dish is barium sauté."

☞ 使用剛開採出來的新鮮鋇，這是豪華殺必死的一道菜。

克莉絲蒂的金臂 2
Kristi Strong-arms 2

 160 km/h

尿壺
urine bottle

 170 km/h

孫子兵法
Sun-Tzu's The Art of War

 180 km/h

交通費
traffic expenses

 140 km/h

麻花辮
plait

 700 km/h

人生
life

061

imposter

［冒充者］

例句

「課長不巧去出差，無法出席會議；
冒充者將會前往參加。」

"My boss can't attend the meeting as he's away on business.
His imposter will attend instead."

☞ 妳就不能說是「代理課長」嗎？

062

urine leakage

［漏尿］

例句

「 不好意思，
請問新宿車站要怎麼走？」
「什麼？你快漏尿出來了？」

"Excuse me. How do I get to Shinjuku Station?"
"Pardon? Urine leakage... what?"

☞ 真是哪壺不開提哪壺。人家都快尿出來了……

063

D-cup
[D罩杯]

例句

要填滿心靈上的空洞，
一定要D罩杯的女性才行！

I badly needed a woman with a D-cup
to fill that hole in my heart.

☞ 這是一定要的啦！

064

Viagra

［威而鋼］

例句

「我要去開幹部會議了。」
「經理，你忘了帶威而鋼。」
「哎呀！」

"I'm off to the board meeting."
"Boss, you forgot your Viagra."
"Oops."

☞ 你這小笨蛋！（笑）

065

Swapping party
［換妻派對］

例句

「請找史蒂芬妮。」
「不好意思，
她去參加換妻派對了。」

"May I speak to Stefanie?"
"I'm afraid she's gone to Swapping party"

☞「要請她回來後打給您嗎？」

066

Lolita complex

［蘿莉控］

例句

課長是排泄狂、雜交者、蘿莉控，
集三位於一體的大變態。

It is said that the section chief is a three-point pervert
who loves scatology, gangbangs, and has a Lolita complex.

☞ 只融你手、只萌你手、七手八腳，夜晚的萬人迷。

067

CHOFERS

［巧菲斯］

例句

「我要烤魚定食，上面加大份的巧菲斯。」
「好的。」

"I'll have the grilled fish set,
along with an extra-large helping of CHOFERS."
"Sure."

☞ 肯定比布丁加泡麵更對味！

068

nose hair

[鼻毛]

例句

「好，痛的時候就像這樣，用鼻毛示意一下就行了。」

"OK, please signal with your nose hair,
like this, when it hurts."

☞ 醫生，你是看個毛啊！

not wearing bras

[沒穿胸罩]

例句

去年車禍意外的受傷者中
有69%都是沒穿胸罩的。

About 69 percent of those injured in traffic accidents last year
were found not wearing bras.

☞ 呃？不穿胸罩就會是凶兆？

pervert

[變態]

例句

「門幫我打開，
因為老子是變態。」

"Please leave the door open
because I am a pervert."

☞ 上帝幫變態開了一扇門，同時還要幫他開一扇窗。

071

Mobile Suit

[機器戰甲]

例句

「課長，有哪裡不對嗎？」
「鮑伯，你的機器戰甲前後穿反了啦！」
「靠！」

"Boss, is there something the matter?"
"Bob, your Mobile Suit is on backwards."
"Oops."

☞ 在被別人發現前，自己早就應該發現N百次了才對啊？

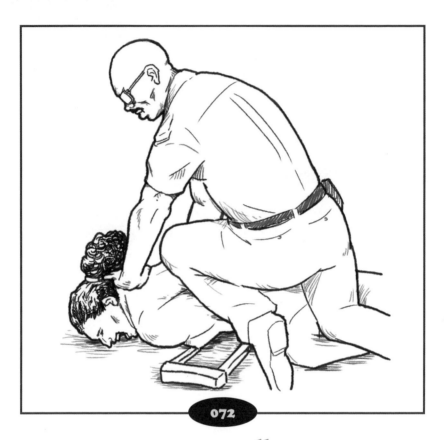

072

moonwalk

[月球漫步]

例句

新手護士克莉絲蒂
在病人看診時用拐杖跳月球漫步，
結果遭到制伏在地。

New nurse Kristi was caught moonwalking
with crutches during medical care.

☞ 咦，到底是誰將她制伏的？醫院裡也有反恐特勤組嗎？

073

handbra

［遮胸］

例句

「全體起立！遮胸！坐下！」

"Everyone rise! Do a handbra! Be seated."

☞「敬禮」喊膩了，不如換個新鮮的吧！

074

fake boobs

［假奶］

例句

在車站內要是有發現任何可疑假奶，
請立即向站長通報。

Please inform the station manager immediately
if you notice any clearly fake boobs in the station.

☞ OMG，人人自危了。

075

torch

［火把］

例句

「要進會議室時，
手上拿著火把比較好。」

"When you enter the conference room,
you should bring a torch."

☞ 到底在開什麼地下會議啊？
我是來開會，不是來探險的！

076

nose hook

［鼻環］

例句

「常務從早上開始
就一直在找他的鼻環。」

The executive managing director
has been looking for a nose hook since this morning.

☞ 找不到它就會被人牽著鼻子走。

077

bloody urine

［血尿］

例句

「回辦公室前，
要不要去喝一杯血尿？」
「好呀！這真是好主意！」

"Don't you want to get some bloody urine
before we go back to the office?"
"Yes, that's a good idea."

☞ 重口味才是真達人！現在大出血特價中。

078

gangbang

［雜交派對］

例句

鮑伯向上司提出
要去參加雜交派對的請假單。

Bob asked his boss for time off
to attend the gangbang.

☞ 別用那種蠟筆小腥的眼神看著我！

079

exhibitionist

［暴露狂］

例句

1945年，
董事長在典禮集會上發表了
〈我以前是個暴露狂〉的有名演說。

In 1945, the chairman delivered his famous
"I was once a flasher" speech at the ceremony.

☞ 像這樣不堪回首的過去還有別的嗎？

克莉絲蒂的金臂 3
Kristi Strong-arms 3

勝負內衣②
special occasion underwears

[註②]想搞定對方時所預先準備的性感內衣。

080

groper

[色狼]

例句

進會議室時，
請注意有沒有色狼。

When you enter the conference room,
watch out for gropers.

☞ 日本也變成穿褲子一定要拉拉鍊的國家了，
連開個會都不能安心。

081

dandruff

［頭皮屑］

例句

「那一大塊白色的東西是什麼？」
「我們公司員工們的頭皮屑。」

"What is that big white chunk?"
"It's my employee dandruff collection."

☞「哇，貴公司真是規模龐大！」

082

dick

［雞雞］

例句

「講到這邊為止有問題嗎？」
「老師，你的雞雞跑出來了。」

"Are there any questions at this point?"
"Um, your dick is hanging out of your underwear."

☞ 不是跑出來，是我放牠出來的。

used toilet paper

[用過的捲筒衛生紙]

例句

「收集用過的捲筒衛生紙，
在國際間已是公認的興趣了。」
赤松氏大聲疾呼。

"Collecting used toilet paper is now an international hobby,"
says Mr. Akamatsu.

☞ 不讓我收集，就捲鋪蓋走人。

084

sex doll

［充氣娃娃］

例句

專務一個疏忽，
就把充氣娃娃留在計程車上了。

The senior managing director carelessly left
his sex doll in the taxi.

☞ 雖然可以理解你的心情，但抱著必死的決心追趕未免也太拚了吧？

085

pubic hair

［陰毛］

例句

「史蒂芬妮怎麼了？為何一臉不爽？」
「燒陰毛沒處理好結果失敗了。」

"Hey Stefanie, why so glum?"
"I tried to burn my pubic hair, but I made a big mess of it."

☞ 失敗了會變成什麼樣？那成功了又會是怎樣？

086

F-cup

［F罩杯］

例句

「F罩杯和精神的關係
就像食物和肉體的關係。」
鮑伯的眼神像血氣方剛的少年一樣熾熱。

"F-cups are to the mind, what food is to the body," said Bob,
his eyes sparkling like a young boy.

☞ 一杯在手，其樂無窮。

087

Tokarev

［托卡列夫手槍］

例句

這把托卡列夫手槍是用100% 再生紙所製成的。

This Tokarev is made from 100% recycled paper.

☞ 對地球友善、對人殘忍的笑容。

088

G-cup

[G罩杯]

例句

古代人認為G罩杯的女性
是幻想出來的生物。

People in the past thought that women with G-cups
were imaginary creatures.

☞ 因為那時娜美還沒出生嘛！

089

Ishihara Corps

[石原軍團③]

例句

NASA決定2018年
要把石原軍團都送到月球上。

NASA plans to send the Ishihara Corps
to the moon by 2018.

☞ 宇宙開發充滿夢想和浪子。

[註③]日本傳奇男星石原裕次郎領軍的藝人組織，多為熱血漢子所組成。

090

three sacred treasures

［三樣神器］

例句

不要用溼溼的手去碰三樣神器，
會造成故障。

Do not touch the three sacred treasures with wet hands.
It can cause them to break.

☞ 你的意思好像是壞了還可以送修嗎？

091

Aron Alpha

［瞬間膠］

例句

東尼在全美瞬間膠賽中拿下優勝，
獲得３公升的瞬間膠。

Tony won the US Aron Alpha blind tasting championship
and received three liters of Aron Alpha.

☞ 可喜可賀！往後半年3秒膠隨你用到爽為止。

092

closet pervert
［沒出櫃的變態］

例句

尼克在會計部中，
是大家都心知肚明沒出櫃的變態。

Within the accounts department,
Nick is viewed with awe as a fucking closet pervert.

☞ 都這麼變態了還沒出櫃，以為大家都瞎了嗎？

093

empty one's bowels

［脫糞］

例句

總裁怪叫一聲衝出他的房間，
結果原地脫糞了。

The president let out a strange noise and shot out of the room,
finally emptying his bowels on the spot.

☞ 然後再返回辦公室繼續開會。

094

morning wood

［晨勃］

例句

董事長50年來第一次晨勃，
因此召開了緊急會議。

An urgent meeting was held because the chairman had
morning wood for the first time in 50 years.

☞ 半世紀以來第一次抬頭，再回首已百年身。

095

school swimwear

[學校泳衣]

例句

現在我們需要的是學校泳衣，
而不是高衩泳衣！

What we need now is school swimwear,
not a T-back.

☞ 你以為這樣說會讓人覺得你很清高嗎？

096

extort

［勒索］

例句

總裁在員工餐廳中
向副總裁勒索一張餐券。

The president extorted a food ticket
from the vice president in the company cafeteria.

☞ 聽說總裁年輕時是出來混的，沒想到現在還在混。

097

exposed breasts

［露奶］

例句

「看見露奶的一瞬間，
我想到許多可以應用在教育上的事情。」
赤松氏大力陳述。

"The moment I saw exposed breasts, I found that
they have many applications for teaching," said Mr. Akamatsu.

☞ 教育就是這樣「喬」出來的。

frequent urination

［頻尿］

例句

「請問新宿車站要怎麼去？」
「什麼？你說你頻尿……」

"Excuse me. How do I get to Shinjuku Station?"
"Pardon? Frequent urination... what?"

☞ 這人不是耳背和嘴賤，而是頭殼壞掉。

099

hostess club

[酒家]

例句

鮑伯對上司一哭二鬧說：
「人家出差時就是想去酒家啦！」

Bob cried and said to his boss,
"I want to go to a hostess club during the business trip."

☞ 一定要喝花酒嗎？喝味噌湯不行嗎？

100

G-spot

［G點］

例句

常務一大早就在找他的G點。

The executive managing director
has been looking for the G-spot since this morning.

☞ 找不到就不能開機了是吧？

常務找東西
The Executive Managing Director Searches In Vain

CHAPTER 3

一般會考的
英文單字

50 ESSENTIAL VOCABULARY
Encounter Rate 80%

101

Ise lobster

［伊勢龍蝦］

例句

「妳幹嘛把伊勢龍蝦放頭上？」
「恁老母今天當班呀！」

"What are you doing with an Ise lobster on your head?"
"It's my turn today."

☞「這位太太！」

102

naked eye

［肉眼］

例句

「人事課的新人表現如何？」
「他的動作太快，肉眼很難看清。」

"How is the new recruit in the personnel section doing?"
"Actually, he moves too fast for the naked eye to see."

☞ 確定是新「人」嗎？

recline one's seat

［椅子向後倒］

例句

「請問法官大人，椅子不能向後倒嗎？」
「被告請不要放太鬆！」

"Your Honor, I can't recline my seat."
"Please do not lounge around in the defendant's seat."

☞ 就算身體放鬆，量刑一樣加重。

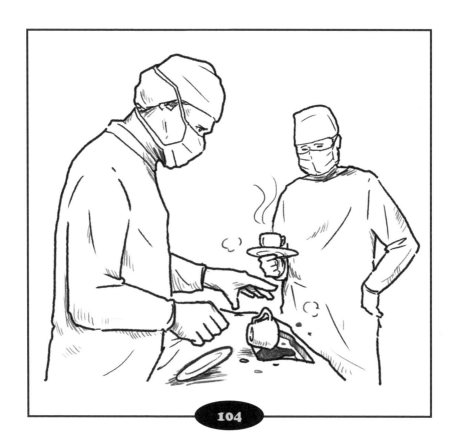

104

cecum

［盲腸］

例句

威廉醫生在開刀時
不小心把咖啡翻倒在盲腸上。

Dr. Williams accidentally spilled coffee on the cecum
during an operation.

☞「快把紗布拿來！」

105

Scotch tape

［膠帶］

例句

鮑伯毫無節制濫用膠帶，
造成公司陷入破產的危機。

Our firm is on the verge of bankruptcy due
to Bob's immeasurable waste of Scotch tape.

☞ 桌子和椅子也都淪陷了⋯⋯

106

raw shrimp

［活跳蝦］

例句

課長的公事包裡，
裝滿夢想和活跳蝦。

The department chief's bag is packed with his dreams
and raw shrimp.

☞ 漏出來了！漏出來了！（指）

107

gastroscope

[胃鏡]

例句

敝公司即將發售業界第一台
附有臉孔辨識功能的照胃鏡。

We are going to release the industry's first gastroscope
with face recognition.

☞ 要是在胃中碰到熟面孔的話，醫生應該會抓狂嚇死。

108

grass and cardboard

［草和厚紙板］

例句

「在那邊吃草和厚紙板的女人是誰？」
「她是總裁的女兒！」

"Who is that lady eating grass and cardboard over there?"
"She is the president's daughter."

☞ 只吃有機食品，果然是總裁千金。

常務找東西 2

The Executive Managing Director Searches In Vain 2

海底
bottom of the sea

MRI

核磁共振攝影
MRI

記得
在那附近…

洞窟
cave

109

massive blackout

［大規模停電］

例句

鮑伯惡意破壞電線，
結果造成首都圈的大規模停電。

Bob damaged the power cables in jest,
and caused a massive blackout in the capital.

☞ 小兵也能立大功？

110

sulk in bed

[輾轉難眠]

例句

停電造成總金額10億美元的經濟損失，
讓鮑伯輾轉難眠。

The blackout caused a total economic loss of one billion dollars
so Bob was sulking in bed.

☞ 但再也沒有來電打擾了……

111

hibernation

［冬眠］

例句

我接到同事來電說
人事部經理從冬眠中醒來了。

I had a call from my colleague to say
that the personnel manager had come out of hibernation.

☞ 說到冬眠，就是熊和人事部經理。

112

arousal

［覺醒］

例句

為了紀念人事部經理的覺醒，
本公司舉辦了睽違83年的新人考試。

To commemorate the arousal,
we will conduct a recruitment exam for the first time in 83 years.

☞ 請問貴公司員工的平均年齡是幾歲啊？

113

behind bars

［坐牢］

例句

「請問齊藤先生在嗎？」
「不好意思，他正在坐牢，
　　明年才會回來。」

"May I speak to Mr. Saito?"
"He is behind bars right now,
and isn't expected back until next year."

☞ 放出來後要請他回電嗎？

114

uncooked barley

［生麥］

例句

「生麥生米生雞蛋！
耶！」

"Uncooked barley, uncooked rice, uncooked egg!
Yeah!"

☞ 你媽怎麼生你的！

115

pacemaker

［心律調節器］

例句

在博愛座附近
請關掉心律調節器。

Please turn off your pacemaker
near the priority seat.

☞ 或是請調到靜音震動模式。

常務找東西 3
The Executive Managing Director Searches In Vain 3

三角旗
pennant

カッパピア 註④

找到了…

[註④]日本群馬縣高崎市的遊樂園名稱。

116

UN Headquarters

［聯合國總部］

例句

我正好經過聯合國總部附近，
就直接殺進來參加安全理事會了。

I happened to pass by the UN Headquarters
and attended the Security Council meeting on the spot.

☞ 乾脆再殺進去提案加入常任理事國好了！

117

defendant

［被告］

例句

「玩笑就開到這裡吧！
現在宣布判決：被告有罪！」

"Joking aside, I will now give my verdict
...I find the defendant guilty!"

☞ 可不可以無罪時再開玩笑啊！

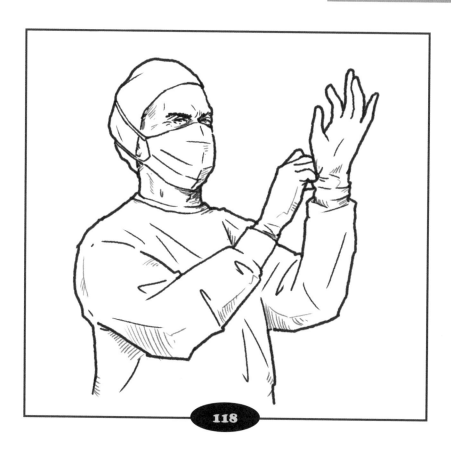

118

encore

［安可］

例句

威廉醫生應觀眾的熱情安可，
再度回到手術室動第二次刀。

Dr. Williams came back into the operating room
for an enthusiastic encore.

☞ 被剖腹的患者一定粉不開心。

119

blow a kiss

［飛吻］

例句

為了維持匯率的穩定，
日本銀行總裁拋出了飛吻。

To stabilize exchange rates,
the Governor of the Bank of Japan blew a kiss.

☞ 寶刀未老，風韻猶存。

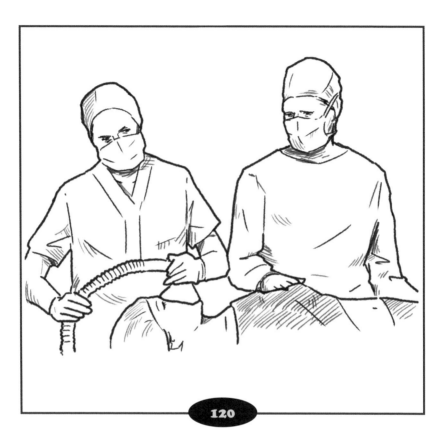

duodenum

［十二指腸］

例句

「醫生，那裡不是十二指腸，是乳頭！」
「靠！」

"Doctor, this isn't the duodenum — it's the nipple."
"Oops."

☞ 拜託先張開眼睛後再動手術啊！

121

accidentally

[意外地]

例句

意外地殺掉了700人，還好用我與生俱來的天真無邪化解了這場危機。

Though I accidentally killed 700 people,
I was able to make up for it with my inherent cheerfulness.

☞ 天真無邪要人命啊！

122

hog farm

[養豬場]

例句

敝公司在日本擁有三間情趣旅館、八家養豬場，本業是文具製造商。

We are a stationary manufacturer with 3 love hotels
and 8 hog farms in Japan.

☞ 我們的新產品是法拉利超跑，開去情趣旅館也拉風！

123

barbed wire

［有刺鐵絲網］

例句

「好漂亮的有刺鐵絲網！」
「謝謝，是我自己編的喔！」

"What nice barbed wire."
"Thank you. I knitted it myself."

☞ 用心親手編出來的倒刺，才能扎進你的肉裡不放。

124

colon fiberscope

［大腸鏡］

例句

這部電影全部都是由大腸鏡
所拍攝出來的。

This movie was filmed entirely
with a colon fiberscope.

☞ 演的是《大腸經》嗎？

125

Shanghai hairy crab

［上海大閘蟹］

例句

「妳怎麼把上海大閘蟹放在頭上？」
「恁老母今天當班啦！」

"What are you doing with a Shanghai hairy crab on your head?"
"It's my turn today."

☞ 哈娃姨上菜。

哈娃姨當班

Mother's Jam-packed Schedule

海龜
marine turtle

126

fall in love

［戀愛］

例句

車掌先生戀愛了，
電車因此誤點2小時。

The train was delayed for more than two hours
because the conductor fell in love.

☞ 延遲証明單是粉紅色的。

127

saury

［秋刀魚］

例句

董事會的報告表示：
卡在老闆喉嚨裡的
秋刀魚刺已經移除了。

The board meeting report says that the saury bone stuck
in the boss's throat was removed.

☞ 大家心頭上的刺也拔掉了。萬歲！

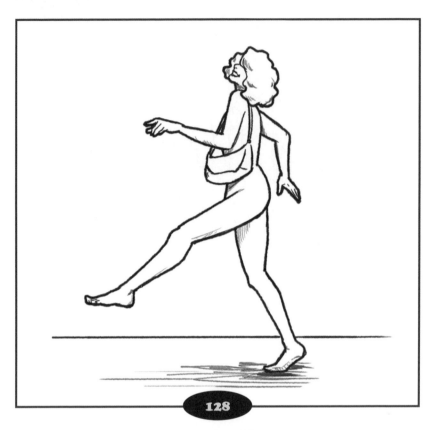

128

morbidly

［病態地］

例句

當我不能集中注意力時就會丟下工作，
全裸地走在大馬路上
病態地高歌。

When I can't focus, I just leave work early
and walk around in the nude singing morbidly.

☞ 為了轉換心情，回歸真我很重要。

129

withdrawal symptoms

［癮頭發作］

例句

請注意：
本電車為防止列車員的
癮頭發作將有緊急停車的狀況。

Caution: train may stop suddenly
in the case of crew's withdrawal symptoms.

☞ 能好好把車停下來就很令人感謝了。

130

brown bear

［棕熊］

例句

福田小姐是第一位徒手
就能殺死棕熊的財務規劃師。

Miss Fukuda is the first financial planner
to kill a brown bear with her bare hands.

☞ 呃，是第一位人類才對吧！

哈娃姨當班 2

Mother's Jam-packed Schedule 2

狗
dog

貓
cat

131

chapped lips

[嘴唇乾裂]

例句

總裁因為嘴唇乾裂，
住院一星期。

Our president has been hospitalized for one week
because the condition of his chapped lips has worsened.

☞ 沒有危及到生命這點倒是令人很慶幸。

132

daily lunch special

［每日特別午餐］

例句

每日特別午餐
可能會有危險的副作用，
所以才會提供優惠的價格。

The daily lunch special can cause dangerous side effects,
so we are offering a special discount.

☞ 優惠和危險經常是一體兩面的啊！

133

love sickness

［愛情病］

例句

總裁因為愛情病住院療養了。

Our president was admitted to hospital
with love sickness.

☞ 嚴重起來還是會死人的……

134

wig

［假髮］

例句

他們舉起假髮互相打招呼。

They saluted each other
by raising their wigs.

☞ 這才是紳士的品格。

135

intensive-care unit

［加護病房］

例句

「我想預約加護病房。」
「您要抽菸的還是禁菸的？」
「抽菸的。」

"I'd like to make a reservation for an intensive-care unit."
"Smoking or Non-Smoking?"
"Smoking please."

☞「槽」點太多，不知從何「吐」起才好……

jump into one's arms

［撲倒懷中］

例句

「 如有疑問，請用力撲倒在我的懷中吧！」
「 現在幾點鐘？」
「 嗚噗！」

"Please jump into my arms if you have any questions."
"Have you got the time?"
"Cough."

☞ 在內臟破裂之前，都儘管用力撲倒在我的懷中吧！

137

dove

［鴿子］

例句

「在那邊對著鴿子熱烈演說的紳士是誰？」
「他是我們的總裁。」

"Who is that gentleman giving a fiery speech
to some doves over there?"
"He is our President."

☞ 真是和平的象徵啊！

138

diarrhea

［拉肚子］

例句

尼克在研修時間一直拉肚子，
後來大家就叫他「尼加拉大瀑布」。

Since having persistent diarrhoea throughout the training period,
Nick has been nicknamed "Niagara."

☞ 這種程度就叫「尼加拉大瀑布」？
未免也太小看世界三大瀑布了吧！

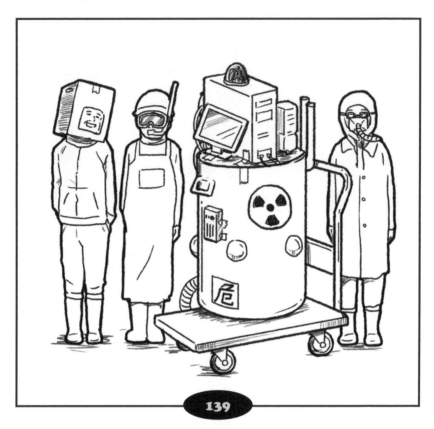

139

nuclear-weapons test

［核試驗］

例句

接下來的節目是……
由六年級男生所帶來的「核試驗」！

Now, the next performance is...
"nuclear-weapons test" by the 6th grade boys!

☞ 真的能確保核能不會外洩嗎？

哈娃姨當班 3
Mother's Jam-packed Schedule 3

熊
bear

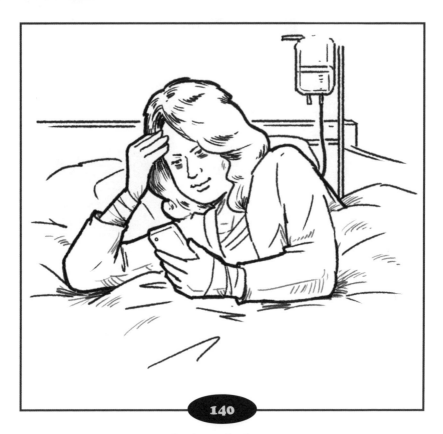

140

liquid diet

［流質食物］

例句

想吃好吃的流質食物，
只有那家醫院才有。

If you want a good liquid diet,
that hospital is the best place in town.

☞ 以成為重病患者為目標！

141

edge of the cliff

［懸崖峭壁］

例句

如有小孩不見的家長，
請前來懸崖峭壁的小孩走失中心。

If you've lost your child, come to our lost child department,
located on the edge of the cliff.

☞ 在找到小孩之前，大人可能會先走丟吧！

shatter

［毀壞］

例句

櫃台小姐一不小心
就把斯洛伐克的經濟全毀了。

The lady at the reception desk
accidentally shattered Slovakia's economy.

☞ 一不小心就可以全毀的斯洛伐克果真是失落法克啊！

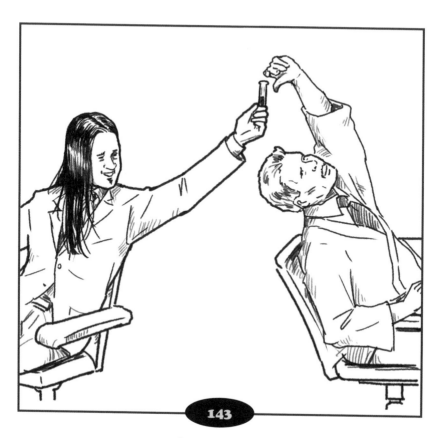

143

plutonium

［鈈］

例句

「可以借我鈈嗎？我忘記帶了。」
「請用！」
「得救了！」

"Can I use your plutonium? I forgot to bring mine."
"Here you are."
"I appreciate it."

☞ 記得省著點用啊！

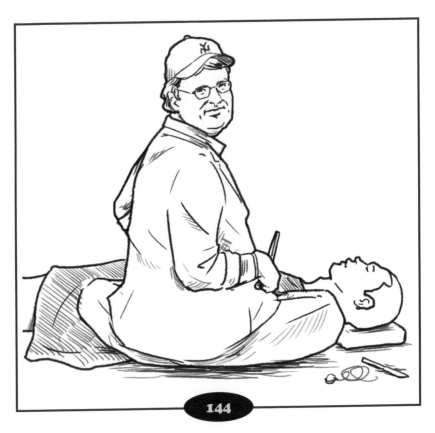

144

heart bypass operation
［心導管手術］

例句

「鮑伯，你從剛才就一直在那裡做什麼？」
「在開心導管手術啊！」

"Bob! What have you been doing with those click-clacks?"
"A heart bypass operation."

☞「開完了一定要收拾乾淨喔！」

145

missile

［飛彈］

例句

「飛彈立刻就要進站，
請大家退到白線後面。」

"The missile is coming.
Please step back behind the white line."

☞ 當列車關門警示音響起，強行進入車廂即有被炸危險。

pressure cooker

[壓力鍋]

例句

史蒂芬妮的母親每天都要
和壓力鍋講上幾小時的話。

Stefanie's mother talks with the pressure cooker
for hours every day.

☞ 這就是壓力鍋會爆炸的原因。

147

groin

［鼠蹊部］

例句

鮑伯的阿公每天一有空
就會自摸鼠蹊部打發時間。

Bob's grandpa spends most of his free time
touching his groin.

☞ 鳥來伯只是想確認鳥還在不在。

148

four-leaf clover

[四葉幸運草]

例句

要申請交通費，
必須附上收據和四葉幸運草。

To claim traffic expenses,
you should submit the bill together with a four-leaf clover.

☞ 可能到地球滅亡都還沒申請到。

half smile

[要笑不笑]

例句

請注意：
搭車時要笑不笑會讓人感覺很噁心。

Please refrain from boarding the train with a half smile,
because it is very creepy.

☞ 假笑和假奶一樣噁心。

150

half smile

［要笑不笑］

例句

請注意：
搭車時要笑不笑會讓人感覺很噁心。

Please refrain from boarding the train with a half smile,
because it is very creepy.

☞ 因為很噁心，所以再提醒一次！

附加例句殺必死
Bonus Sentences

玩弄乳頭 fiddle with nioole
例句 Stefanie was caught fiddling with her boss's nipple during the presentation.
史蒂芬妮企圖在發表報告時玩弄上司的乳頭，結果被制伏在地。

乳環 areola
例句 His name is familiar, but his areola doesn't ring any bells.
我對他的名字是有印象，但是看到他的乳環卻怎麼也想不起來。

雷神 Thunder
例句 "Bob makes it seem like he is eating Thunder, but actually he is eating NOUGAT CHOCOLATE."
「鮑伯裝作他在吃雷神，其實吃的是七七乳加巧克力。」

惡劣玩笑 prank
例句 As a result of Bob's prank, more than 87000 houses collapsed and 340000 were made homeless.
鮑伯開了一個惡劣玩笑，結果害8萬7千間民宅倒塌、34萬人無家可歸。

辦趴部長 party animal
例句 I have worked as a party animal at my company since completing my Bachelor of physics in 1999.
我在1999年拿到物理學的學位後，就在敝公司擔任辦趴部長。

髮線 hairline
例句 I like watching his hairline recede.
我最喜歡觀察他的髮線後退。

流彈 stray bullet
例句 Stray bullets are our biggest seller.
流彈是敝公司的主力商品之一。

雷杖 thunder rod
例句 I found an Indonesian company that specializes in thunder rods.
我找到一家專門銷售雷杖的印尼公司。

叢林 jungle
例句 The department manager discovered the manager deep in jungle and brought him back to Japan.
部門經理在密林深處找到了經理，將他帶回日本。

迎擊 intercept
例句 It is said that the accountant general's daughter intercepts short-range missiles on Mondays.
據說星期一時會計課長的女兒用短距離飛彈迎頭痛擊。

喉結 Adam's apple
例句 Please refrain from touching the department manager's Adam's apple when your hands are dirty.
請不要用沾滿泥巴的手摸部門經理的喉結。

貧民區 inner city
例句 The manager was brought up in the inner city and lived there until he was 41.
經理在41歲以前，都一直生長在貧民區。

網子 net
例句 A decade ago, our president found Bob entangled in a net off the coast, and brought him back to the office.
10年前，總裁在海岸邊發現了被網子纏住的鮑伯，就把他帶回了公司。

三角褲 panties
例句 Stefanie was caught removing her panties during the presentation.
史蒂芬妮在發表報告中想脫下三角褲，結果被制伏在地。

鼻屎 booger
例句 The executive managing director used all his remaining strength to put a booger on Stefanie.
常務用盡最後的力量，把鼻屎黏在史蒂芬妮的身上。

半裸 semi-naked
例句 The board members work semi-naked to cut down on costs.
因為削減經費，員工們只好半裸著上班。

痂 scab
例句 "What material is enclosed?" "Just Bob's freshly picked scab."
「資料袋裡裝的是什麼？」「鮑伯剛剝下來的痂。」

色迷迷 lecherous nature
例句 The cause of the tragedy was the managing director's lecherous nature.
都怪常務色迷迷，結果引發了慘事。

短跑起跑姿勢 crouch start
例句 "Let's have a crouch start tonight. I found a good athletics field near the station."
「今晚一起練短跑起跑姿勢吧！我發現車站附近有一個不錯的田徑場。」

脫脂棉 absorbent cotton
例句 My husband and I met through our mutual interest in collecting used absorbent cotton.
我和老公是因為喜歡收集用過的脫脂棉才認識的。

費洛蒙 pheromone
例句 Recently, the manager's sex pheromones are worrying grape growers in Matsumoto, Nagano Prefecture.
最近，經理散發出的性費洛蒙，讓長野縣松本市的葡萄栽培農家很苦惱。

很長的陰毛 long public hair
例句 "What happened to your knee?" "I tripped over a long pubic hair." "Again?"
「你的膝蓋怎麼了？」「陰毛太長害我絆倒。」「又來了！」

培根蛋麵 carbonara
例句 The world's oldest carbonara fossil was found in a layer of rock from the early Jurassic period.
從侏儸紀前期的岩層中發現世界最古老的培根蛋麵化石。

胃液 gastric juice
例句 "I'm sorry, but I spilled my gastric juice over the contract." "It's absolutely fine."
「抱歉，胃液灑到合約上了。」「沒關係。」

失禁 incontinent
例句 Well, I just realized that I've been incontinent forty-three times this week.
好吧，我現在才發現這禮拜失禁了43次。

乳頭 nipple
例句 Bob's nipples look like dots from a distance.
鮑伯的乳頭遠看過去就是兩粒小點。

變裝 drag
例句 The director of fire management lashed out at the CEO, yelling "What's wrong with dressing in drag?"
火災管理部經理衝著CEO大吼：「變裝哪裡不對了？」

包莖 phimosis
例句 The director of fire management lashed out at the CEO, yelling "What's wrong with phimosis?"
火災管理部經理衝著CEO大吼：「包莖哪裡不好了？」

蘿莉控 Lolita complex
例句 The director of fire management lashed out at the CEO, yelling "What's wrong with having a Lolita complex?"
火災管理部經理衝著CEO大吼：「蘿莉控哪裡不行了？」

SM S&M
例句 The director of fire management lashed out at the CEO, yelling "What's wrong with S&M?"
火災管理部經理衝著CEO大吼：「SM哪裡不OK？」

✄ 正面為英文與ＫＫ音標發音，反面為中文
定義與頁數標示。

✄ 建議大家可將單字卡沿線剪下，方便隨身
攜帶增加記憶力。

accidentally [ˌæksə`dɛnt!ɪ]	**arousal** [ə`raʊz!]
anus [`enəs]	**balls** [bɔls]
areola [ə`rɪələ]	**barbed wire** [bɑrbd waɪr]
army crawl [`ɑrmɪ krɔl]	**barium** [`bɛrɪəm]
Aron Alpha	**behind bars** [bɪ`haɪnd bɑrz]

"Please leave the door open because I am a pervert."

「 門幫我打開，因為老子是個變態。 」

big rod [bɪg rɑd]	**bungee** [ˋbʌndʒɪ]
blindfold sex [ˋblaɪndˌfold sɛks]	**cecum** [ˋsikəm]
bloody urine [ˋblʌdɪ ˋjʊrɪn]	**chainsaw** [tʃen sɔ]
bloomers [ˋblumɚs]	**chapped lips** [tʃæpt lɪps]
blow a kiss [blo ə kɪs]	**char siu** [tʃɑr ʃu]
bottom cleavage [ˋbatəmˋklivɪdʒ]	**chest hair** [tʃɛst hɛr]
briefs [brifs]	**CHOFERS**
brown bear [braʊn bɛr]	**closet pervert** [ˋklazɪt pəˋvɚt]

colon fiberscope [ˈkolənˈfaɪbəˌskop]	**diarrhea** [ˌdaɪəˈriə]
completely naked [kəmˈplitlɪ ˈnekɪd]	**dick** [dɪk]
condom [ˈkɑndəm]	**dine and dash** [daɪn ænd dæʃ]
cosplay [ˈkɑsple]	**dirty joke** [ˈdɝtɪ dʒok]
daily lunch special [ˈdelɪ lʌntʃ spɛʃəl]	**dove** [dʌv]
dandruff [ˈdændrəf]	**dump** [dʌmp]
D-cup [di kʌp]	**duodenum** [ˌdjuəˈdinəm]
defendant [dɪˈfɛndənt]	**edge of the cliff** [ɛdʒ ɔf ðə klɪf]

emiction [ɪˋmɪkʃən]	**fake boobs** [fek bubs]
empty one's bowels [ˋɛmptɪ wʌnsˋ bauəlz]	**fall in love** [fɔl ɪn lʌv]
encore [ˋaŋkor]	**fart** [fɑrt]
erection [ɪˋrɛkʃən]	**F-cup** [ɛf kʌp]
erogenous zone [ɪˏradʒənəs ˋzon]	**four-leaf clover** [for lif ˋklovɚ]
exhibitionist [ˏɛksəˋbɪʃənɪst]	**frequent urination** [ˋfrikwənt ˏjurəˋneʃən]
exposed breast [ɪkˋspozd brɛst]]	**fuck buddy** [fʌk ˋbʌdɪ]
extort [ɪkˋstort]	**gangbang** [ˋgæŋˏbæŋ]

假奶 P.86	排尿 P.40
戀愛 P.144	脫糞 P.106
屁 P.49	安可 P.135
F 罩杯 P.52 / P.99	勃起 P.34
四葉幸運草 P.168	性感帶 P.17
頻尿 P.111	暴露狂 P.91
炮友 P.44	露奶 P.110
雜交派對 P.90	勒索 P.109

garter belt [ˈɡɑrtə bɛlt]		**handbra** [hændbrɑ]
gastroscope [ˈɡæstrəˌskop]		**hangnail** [ˈhæŋˌnel]
G-cup [dʒi kʌp]		**headspin** [hɛdspɪn]
grass and cardboard [ɡræs ænd ˈkɑrdˌbord]		**heart bypass operation** [hɑrt ˈbaɪˌpæs ˌɑpəˈreʃən]
groper [ɡropə-]		**hibernation** [ˌhaɪbə-ˈneʃən]
groin [ɡrɔɪn]		**hog farm** [hɑɡ fɑrm]
G-spot [dʒi spɑt]		**horny** [ˈhɔrnɪ]
half smile [hæf smaɪl]		**hostess club** [ˈhostɪs klʌb]

imposter [ɪmˈpostɚ]	**love sickness** [lʌv ˈsɪknɪs]
intensive-care unit [ɪnˈtɛnsɪv kɛr ˈjunɪt]	**Mario Kart**
Ise lobster	**masochist** [ˈmæzəkɪst]
Ishihara Corps	**massive blackout** [ˈmæsɪv ˈblækˌaʊt]
jump into one's arms [dʒʌmp ˈɪntu wʌns ɑrmz]	**missile** [ˈmɪs!]
Kafrizzle [kɑˈfrɪz!]	**military advisor** [ˈmɪləˌtɛrɪ ədˈvaɪzɚ]
liquid diet [ˈlɪkwɪd ˈdaɪət]	**mistress** [ˈmɪstrɪs]
Lolita complex	**Mobile Suit** [ˈmobɪl sut]

mole hair [mol hɛr]	**nose hook** [noz hʊk]
moonwalk [ˋmunˌwɔk]	**ot wearing bras** [nɑt ˋwɛrɪŋ brɑs]
morbidly [ˋmɔrbɪdlɪ]	**nuclear-weapons test** [ˋnjuklɪɚ ˋwɛpəns tɛst]
morning wood [ˋmɔrnɪŋ wʊd]	**pacemaker** [ˋpesˌmekɚ]
naked eye [ˋnekɪd aɪ]	**panty line** [ˋpæntɪ laɪn]
nipple [ˋnɪpl̩]	**Patriot missile** [ˋpetrɪət ˋmɪsl̩]
nipple cover [ˋnɪpl̩ ˋkʌvɚ]	**pee** [pi]
nose hair [noz hɛr]	**pervert** [pɚˋvɝt]

pillow talk [ˈpɪlo tɔk]	**raise an army** [rez ænˈɑrmɪ]
pink rotor [pɪŋk ˈrotɚ]	**raw shrimp** [rɔ ʃrɪmp]
plutonium [pluˈtonɪəm]	**recline one's seat** [rɪˈklaɪn wʌns sit]
ponzu sauce	**run around naked** [ˈrʌn əˌraʊnd naked]
pressure cooker [ˈprɛʃɚ ˈkʊkɚ]	**sakura shrimp**
public hair [ˈpʌblɪk hɛr]	**salmon carpaccio** [ˈsæmən karpatNjo]
quadruple jump [ˈkwɑdrʊp! dʒʌmp]	**saury** [ˈsɔrɪ]
rain dance [ren dæns]	**school swimwear** [skul ˈswɪmˌwɛr]

Scotch tape [skatʃ tep]	**shatter** [`ʃætə·]
sensitive spot [`sɛnsətɪv spat]	**stamp with blood** [stæmp wɪð blʌd]
sex doll [`sɛks dɑl]	**STD** **Sexually** **Transmitted Disease**
sexily [`sɛksɪlɪ]	**sulk in bed** [sʌlk ɪn bɛd]
sexual slave [`sɛkʃʋəl slev]	**Swapping party** [swapɪŋ `partɪ]
sexual position [`sɛkʃʋəl pə`zɪʃən]	**three sacred treasures** [θri `sekrɪd `trɛʒə·]
sexual propensity [`sɛkʃʋəl prə`pɛnsətɪ]	**Thunder** [`θʌndə·]
Shanghai hairy crab [`ʃæŋhaɪ `hɛrɪ kræb]	**Tokarev**

●	**torch** [tɔrtʃ]	●	**urine leakage** [ˈjʊrɪn ˈlikɪdʒ]
●	**Viagra**	●	**used toilet paper** [juzd ˈtɔɪlɪt ˈpepɚ]
●	**uncooked barley** [ʌnˈkʊkt ˈbarlɪ]	●	**wig** [wɪg]
●	**UN Headquarters** [ju ɛn ˈhɛdˈkwɔrtɚz]	●	**withdrawal symptoms** [wɪðˈdrɔəl ˈsɪmptəm]
●	**urine bottle** [ˈjʊrɪn ˈbatl]	●	**women issues** [ˈwɪmɪn ˈɪʃʊs]

After taking a dump at work, Stefanie doesn't flush the toilet on purpose.

史蒂芬妮在公司裡故意不把大便沖掉。

"Boss, you have a call on line 2 from your fuck buddy."
"Thank you, put her through."

「課長，2線是你炮友打來的。」
「好的，請接過來。」